ELMER
and the Stranger

David McKee

Andersen Press

Elmer, the patchwork elephant, had just started his morning walk when Tiger arrived.

"Elmer," he said, "there's a stranger around and he's acting very strangely. He jumps and falls over."

"Strangers often act strangely; that's why they're strangers," said Elmer.

"Well I don't think he's happy," said Tiger.

This ELMER book belongs to:

. . . .

For Fabio B and Amy Z

This paperback edition first published in 2009 by Andersen Press Ltd.
First published in Great Britain in 2000 by Andersen Press Ltd.,
20 Vauxhall Bridge Road, London SW1V 2SA.
Published in Australia by Random House Australia Pty.,
Level 3, 100 Pacific Highway, North Sydney, NSW 2060.
Copyright © David McKee, 2000.
The rights of David McKee to be identified as the author and illustrator
of this work have been asserted by him in accordance with
the Copyright, Designs and Patents Act, 1988.
All rights reserved.
Colour separated in Switzerland by Photolitho AG, Zürich.
Printed and bound in China.

10   9   8   7   6   5   4

British Library Cataloguing in Publication Data available.

ISBN 978 1 84939 138 2 (Book People edition)
ISBN 978 1 84270 785 2 (Trade paperback edition)
ISBN 978 1 84270 782 1 (paperback and CD edition)

This book has been printed on acid-free paper

Just then Lion appeared. "Hello, Elmer.
Hello, Tiger," he said.
"Elmer, there's a strange chap around. He sort of . . .
sort of . . ."
"Jumps," said Tiger. "Elmer knows."

"And then he kind of . . . well he . . ."
"Falls over," finished Tiger. "Elmer knows."
"Yes, well also he seems . . . aah . . ."
"Unhappy," said Tiger. "Elmer knows."
"Let's just go and see," said Elmer kindly.

Soon they came to a clearing.
"This is where he usually jumps," said Tiger.
"And falls over," added Lion. "And here he comes."
With huge bounces, into the clearing came a kangaroo.
Then he stopped, hesitated, and fell over. He picked
himself up and sobbed, "I'm a failure."
"Not a happy chappy," said Lion.
"Let's talk to him," said Elmer.

"Hello," said Elmer. "What's the matter?"
"Hello," Kangaroo sniffed. "I can't jump.
When I try to, I fall over. We're going to have
a jumping competition and I came here to
practise, secretly. But it's no use. I can't jump.
I'll be laughed at."

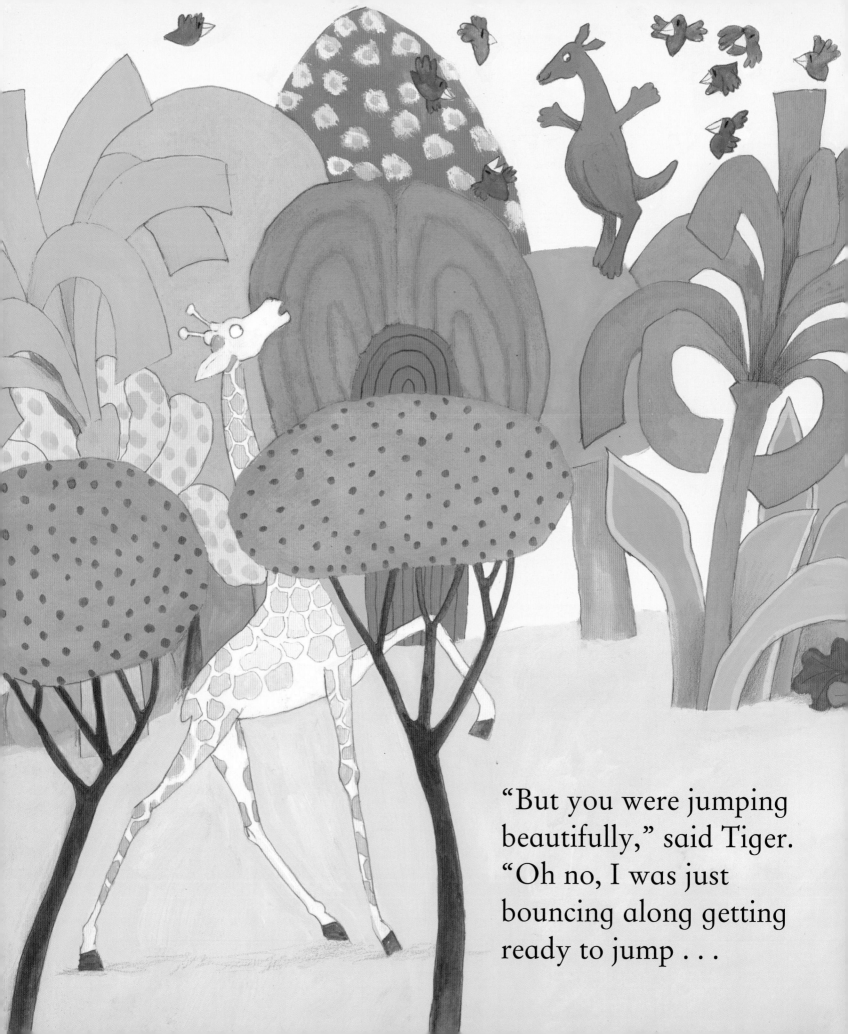

"But you were jumping beautifully," said Tiger. "Oh no, I was just bouncing along getting ready to jump . . .

I'm a good bouncer," said Kangaroo and, to prove it, bounced higher than Giraffe who happened to be passing. "Very impressive," said Tiger. "But when I think about the jump I fall over," sighed Kangaroo. "This needs some thought," said Elmer. "We'll be back tomorrow."

Kangaroo laughed, and with an
enormous bounce landed beside
Lion and Tiger.

"Fantastic jump," said Tiger.
"You mean 'bounce'," said Kangaroo. "I can't jump." Lion chuckled. "A bounce IS a jump."
"Lion's right," said Elmer. "Forget jumping, just bounce. Now, let's go to that competition!"

Kangaroo led the way, delighted that his new friends were going with him. They arrived just as the competition began.

After a while, Elmer said, "Come on, Kangaroo, it's time you had a go."
There was a roar of applause as a white kangaroo made an enormous jump.
"That will be hard to beat," said Kangaroo.

Elmer whispered to Lion and Tiger. They grinned and went to stand just past the spot where the white kangaroo had landed. As Kangaroo was getting ready, Elmer said, "Drat! We'll get our feet wet."

Kangaroo gave a laugh, and with an enormous bounce once again landed beside Lion and Tiger.

That jump won the competition.

Later, Kangaroo thanked Elmer, Lion and Tiger for their help.
"You made me remember the river," he said. "I didn't think about jumping."

When they were back home, Lion said, "Strange thing, I felt that we were the . . . aah . . ."

"Strangers," finished Tiger.

"Yes," laughed Elmer. "And now we're all . . . aah . . ."

"Friends!" they laughed together.

Read more ELMER stories

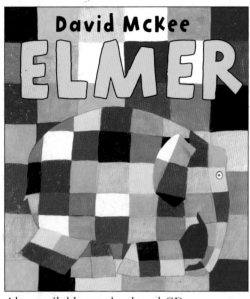

Also available as a book and CD

Also available as a book and CD

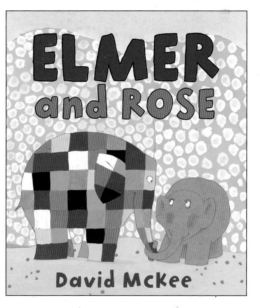

Also available as a book and CD